King of the Beasties

Adapted by Ann Braybrooks
Illustrated by Darrell Baker

 A GOLDEN BOOK • NEW YORK
Golden Books Publishing Company, Inc., New York, New York 10106

One day, while he was looking at pictures of wild animals, Tigger realized that he was related to the lion, the king of beasts. "I must be a king, too!" said Tigger.

"We don't need a king," said Owl.

"Well, what if a wild jagular was on the loose?" Tigger asked. "Who would protect you?"

"Hmmm," said Pooh.

Tigger had a plan. He stopped by Rabbit's house
when Rabbit wasn't home and borrowed a tablecloth,
a pillow, and a broom.

Then, using Rabbit's things, Tigger made a
fierce-looking jagular and hung it from a tree.
"I don't want to scare 'em too much," he said
to himself. "I just want 'em to make me king!"

Soon, when everyone came near, Tigger began
to bounce up and down. "Jagular! Jagular!" he cried.
"Run for your lives!"

Tigger ran up to the jagular and gave it a few fierce whacks with a stick. Then he tossed the jagular into a cage.

"Hurray for Tigger!" cried Pooh. "He saved us! Tigger *should* be king!"

And so, just as he had wanted, Tigger was crowned
King of the Hundred-Acre Wood.
He began acting like a king right away.

"First of all," commanded King Tigger, "from now on and forever after the Hundred-Acre Wood shall be known as Tiggeropolis!"

Next King Tigger commanded his subjects to paint
the trees in Tiggeropolis royal orange and black!

Then he ordered everyone to bounce.
"But my feet are tired from all that painting,"
Pooh complained.

Without saying a word, Tigger pointed to the caged
jagular. Pooh quickly began to bounce. He knew he
should not argue with a king!

Later Rabbit wandered by. "Hmmm," he said to himself. "That looks like my tablecloth. And that's my pillow! If Tigger wanted to borrow my things, he should have asked. I'll teach that Tigger a lesson!"

Rabbit grabbed the jagular, left a note in its place, and went home.

Soon Owl came by and saw the note. He read it to King Tigger.

"I've freed my friend and taken him with me. Signed, Another Jagular."

"Oops!" Tigger muttered under his breath. "This *new* jagular is probably *real*!" So he sounded the alarm. "Everyone head for the hills!" he yelled.

But Pooh just stood there scratching his head. "Shouldn't we try to capture the jagular?" he asked.

"You'll have to protect us, King Tigger!" Piglet added.

"You're right," answered Tigger, gulping. "Okay. Everybody follow me."

The jagular's tracks led straight to Rabbit's house.
Tigger burst through the door.

"It's the jagular!" he shouted, pouncing on the beast.

"Tigger!" Rabbit yelled. "That's my *tablecloth*!"

"It is?" said Tigger, embarrassed. "Oh, so it is. But don't forget," he added, "there's still that *other* jagular out there—the one who wrote the note!"

"There *is* no other jagular!" Rabbit declared. "*I* wrote the note."

"I don't understand, King Tigger," said
Piglet in a small voice.

Tigger hung his head. "I've got a confession to make," he said. "I made up the jagular because I wanted so much to be king. I guess I got carried away." He sniffed. "I'm sorry."

"I suppose we could forgive you, Tigger," Piglet said. "After all, you *are* our friend."

"That's right!" said Tigger, looking around happily. "I'm your friend."

"But what about all that painting and bouncing?"
Pooh asked.

"I promise I won't ever do that stuff again!"
declared Tigger. "C'mon, let's have a king
*un*crowning!"

Afterward the former king declared, "I feel like a new Tigger! A bouncier Tigger! Even if I'm not king, I'm still Tigger!"

"That's true," said Rabbit with a sigh.

Tigger grinned. "And I'm the only one!"